I Remember Grandpa

I REMEM

BER GRANDPA

A Story by Truman Capote

Illustrated by Barry Moser

PEACHTREE PUBLISHERS, LTD.

Published by
PEACHTREE PUBLISHERS, LTD.
494 Armour Circle, N.E.
Atlanta, Georgia 30324

Manufactured in the United States of America

1st printing

Library of Congress Catalog Card Number 87-80965

ISBN 0-934601-22-4

The illustrations in this book were executed with watercolor on Royal Watercolor Society Paper, made by
hand in 1982 by J. Barcham Green, England.

The text type was set in Bembo by Typo–Repro Service, Inc., Atlanta, Georgia.

The calligraphy was done by Barry Moser of Pennyroyal Press, West Hatfield, Massachusetts.

Printed by Rose Printing Company, Tallahassee, Florida.

Design by Barry Moser.

I REMEMBER GRANDPA

O NE of the saddest days of my life was when I left my boyhood home in the foothills of the West Virginia Allegheny Mountains. My Ma and Pa and I lived with my Grandma and Grandpa in a little wooden cottage about a mile from the nearest road and thirty miles from the nearest town. Our home had been handed down from generation to generation, or so my Grandpa told me. We had always been one family but because of my coming of school age, my Pa decided, for all of us, to move to Virginia, somewhere over the mountains, and leave Grandpa and Grandma in the care of a new worker of our land.

I'll never forget the days before we left. The time of the year was Indian Summer, the leaves were turning from their dull green color to flashing shades of orange, red, yellow, and purple. Autumn stillness was in the air. Grandpa was listless because he knew that something was amiss. He had become quiet and pouting, like he always did when something was wrong and no one told him what it was. When the problem became serious enough, as it always did, he would finally learn of it; and then he would pull me up on his lap, get me comfortable, and tell me what he thought of the situation.

"Bobby," he said one Friday night, "I've got a secret I want to share with you someday." He looked down at the ground and made quick little patterns in the sand with his toes. It was getting chilly because night was approaching and the sand must have felt warm. I kept looking at his face, searching for his eyes, but they wouldn't move, just stared blankly at his bare feet. "You'll be leaving here soon. I'm going to miss you when you go. You'll be around strange people and I want you to remember me and my secret. Come back someday and we'll share it together." He looked at me then and he was so sad. I couldn't understand at all then what he meant by a secret and I wanted to hear more. Tears came to his eyes and I knew that his heart must have been breaking. I just sat there, immobilized; I'd never seen him cry. In a most pitiful voice, my Grandpa asked, "You will come back someday, won't you?" I hugged him and told him how I would; how I could never forget him and Grandma.

I asked Ma that night who had told Grandpa that I was leaving. She said we all were going, the first of next week. She explained that Pa had found out in town that I could yet be enrolled in school for the next year—if we moved right away. She said we would be living on another farm with a furnished home and we would leave everything here with Grandpa and Grandma. We would be taking only our clothes and the car. Ma said we would be leaving Monday. Just two more days—it seemed impossible, like a dream. Even Grandma wasn't the same, quiet and moping around the house. No one said anything to her about our going. I said

Grandpa was listless because he knew that something was amiss. He had become quiet and pouting, like he always did when something was wrong and no one told him what it was.

nothing because Ma firmly instructed me that it would make matters worse. She told me that she would tell Grandma, in her own way, in her own time.

Saturday came. We had just finished dinner, Grandma and Ma were clearing the table and I wanted to be by myself for a while. Pa said something about checking the car and he set out for the old smokehouse where, along with all our meat, he kept the tools and spare parts for the car. My favorite spot for being alone was down by the creek where the butter and milk were stored in the coolness of the fresh spring water. On the way I couldn't help thinking, "Just one more day." It was such a short time. I wondered what it would be like on Monday, Tuesday, or Wednesday, when we wouldn't be around.

I arrived at the creek and there sat Grandpa, smoking his pipe and watching the water glide over the rocks, making little ripples, catching a twig here and there. The cattails rocked back and forth when a little wind came along; I don't think I can remember one time when I came here and the wind wasn't blowing. Grandpa was just watching the water spinning in little circles, flowing endlessly around the bend and out of sight. I always came here when I wanted to be alone; I'd cried here a lot too: when Nelly, one of our milk cows, died; when Grandma got the fever and laid around and suffered for days. Pa had to go for the doctor and Grandpa didn't know what to do, he prayed a lot and Preacher Thomas came around and did what he could. He sure helped Grandma, with his fancy praying and all. He stayed by her bedside for one whole day. One time she almost left us but Preacher Thomas held her hand real tight. He made me leave the room. I went down to the creek and cried like I

6 could never quit. I couldn't figure out such misery and why people had to get sick, lay and suffer so, and why sometimes they died.

Grandpa hadn't seen me yet and I thought I'd surprise him. I really couldn't sneak up on anyone anyway, especially Grandpa. He turned around just as I was going to yell at him. He motioned for me to sit down beside him and started on another of his lying spells but they weren't the usual funny or make-believe stories he told when he was relaxing. He told me again of the secret he would share with me someday. He told me how people, when they're apart from each other, tend to forget each other. He told me how he was going to miss me and my Mother and Father when we were gone. He made me promise I would write every week and let him know how I was doing. "Well, I can't write very good. I ain't been to no school yet, you know," I remember telling him. Grandpa had taught me to write as much as I could. Pa was always so busy working the fields and bringing the money in. I'll never forget some of the arguments Pa and Grandpa used to get into—Pa yelling about me going to school and Grandpa telling how he could learn me all that was necessary and important. I always had wondered, though, what was on the other side of those mountains. Grandpa never could tell me that. Sometimes Pa and I would go into town to get food and stuff, we never went further than that.

Grandpa told me our secret wouldn't be any good unless the both of us kept our promises. He promised to answer my letters each week and would keep my picture on his bureau top in his and Grandma's bedroom, along with Grandma's and Ma's and Pa's pictures. I still remember the day all of us took Grandma into town for her and my pictures. The car

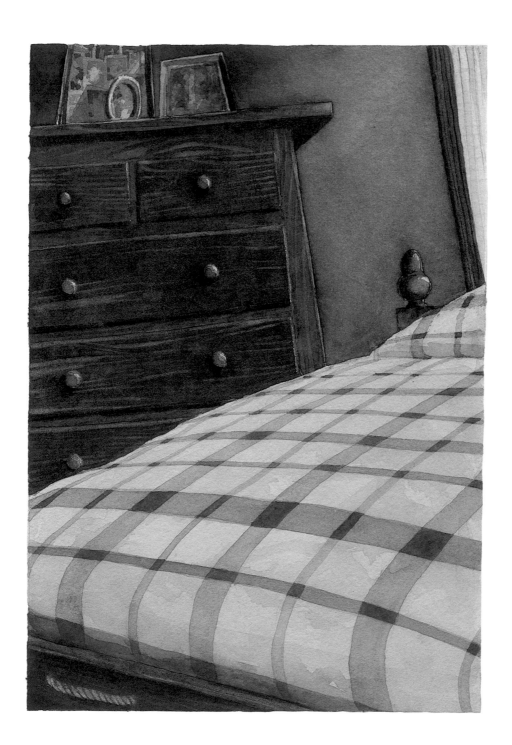

He promised to answer my letters each week and would keep my picture on his bureau top in his and Grandma's bedroom, along with Grandma's and Ma's and Pa's pictures.

broke down and Grandma was all upset by the time we got to
the pictureman. She was fuming and fussing and didn't even
smile when the pictureman exploded the powder. She made
up with Grandpa, though, and on the way home they snug-
gled up to each other and made me feel so good inside. That
scowling picture was put in the frame with the rest of
the pictures.

My Grandpa and I sat together by the creek all evening.
He told me I would be growing up away from him. He told
me to trust and obey my Ma and Pa; to believe in God and go
to church every Sunday. Even when I didn't feel like it. He
made me promise I would go to church with him and
Grandma tomorrow—if he could get her to go—and he made
me promise to go with my Ma and Pa in our new home and
when I was big enough, to take them with me to church. He
told me he was worried about Grandma. "She sure hates to
see your Ma go," he said. "She sure got a strange look in her
eyes when Ma told her this morning. Somehow she just can't
believe it. It seems females need other female companionship
more than men do. I don't know though. It sure is tearing her
up. I think she's going to be sick—awful sick."

Everyone was long-faced at the supper table Saturday
night. The two men were talking about the farmer moving in
the first of the week. Pa said something about turning the
papers to the land over to the new man. His room would be
free and he would get a percentage from the land for working
it. Grandma and Grandpa would get the rest to live off of. Pa
did most of the talking and Grandpa just sat there and agreed.
I'd have sworn Grandpa had aged two years in those few days
and I still don't think he really knew what was happening.
They talked about the car and Grandpa seemed to think that

slow driving in second gear up the mountains would be best. He said that the cool autumn air would keep the engine heat down.

Grandma just picked at her food and pushed it back and forth on her plate, like she was looking for something in it. Her head was bowed, like when she went to church and prayed. Maybe she was praying then, I couldn't see her eyes. Ma reached over and very gently put her hand on Grandma's. "Do you want to go to bed now?" Ma asked her and Grandma started crying softly, tears dripping down on her plate and all over her beautiful crimson dress she was wearing just for us because she knew we were leaving on Monday. I think she'd worn it just one other time—when Preacher Thomas died the Christmas before. I remember Grandpa arguing something about a bright dress at a funeral but Grandma wore it just the same. She said it was still new and clean and she wasn't ashamed of it. Grandpa knew when he was licked and he shut up.

Ma took Grandma into her bedroom and Grandpa went out onto the porch. Pa just put his head down on his arms and was very still, like he was asleep. I couldn't eat anymore and I felt awful inside, like I wanted to die. I went out on the porch with Grandpa. A few crickets could still be heard and a cool breeze tingled the skin, making you think of pumpkins, haystacks, Thanksgiving, Christmas, and snow. I wondered if they had things like that in Virginia.

Grandpa was sitting in the old rocking chair, the one Grandma liked so much, just rocking back and forth, looking straight into the sky, blinking his eyes now and then. "Snow clouds coming early this year," he was saying. "Look pretty thick and this wind don't feel so good." He didn't pull me

He told me he was worried about Grandma. "She sure hates to see your Ma go," he said. "She sure got a strange look in her eyes when Ma told her this morning. Somehow she just can't believe it."

onto his lap this time. Maybe he thought I was getting too big 13

for that. "You know," he began his storytelling again, "your Father has worked this land by himself for the last five years. It's been in the family for over seventy or eighty years. I was hoping you would work it next. Now some foreigner's coming in and who knows what'll happen. Boy, I sure can't figure it out. How stubborn your Father can be. Just up and leaving us like this. Don't seem right. Isn't fair."

The sound of scraping dishes could now be heard. A sudden gush of cold air discouraged me from staying outdoors any longer. Ma was washing the dishes and pointing to a large container of hog slop, larger than usual because no one ate much for supper. "Take this to the hogs before it gets any darker and we have some weather. And don't be making any noise around here tonight, your grandmother's sick," she told me. Ma was her old self anyway. "Do you hear?" she asked and I could see she had been crying; her eyes were red and she looked real tired.

Pa kept five hogs a little distance from the house. Squealing loudly and jumping all over the place. They sure were fat and I hated missing butchering time this year. The new people would get all the new fresh meat. I thought of the new man that would move in, if he'd have a family or not. I guessed that they would take Ma and Pa's room. Looking around the land a few minutes I remembered so clearly the many hours and days Pa labored in these fields. There were five of them that I could see from where I was. We owned two of them; these would go to the new man. On these we grew potatoes and some corn and peas. I remember one year Ma set out some strawberries. It was going to be a surprise to Pa. Well, Pa dug them up. Said they were the funniest-looking weeds he'd ever seen. You should've seen Ma's face when Pa came running into the house telling her of his find. I don't know where Ma got all those names she called Pa that day.

Two other fields were just grass and thistle. Pa said he had tried to buy them but the owner won't sell. Pa seemed to think the owner was waiting to buy up Pa's land. The last piece of land, that cleared stretch running up the valley, was where Pa made his money planting potatoes and corn—all by hand, and selling it to the people in town. Pa didn't believe in modern machinery, but he did say, just a few months before, that if he had to work much longer in these fields, he was going to get some machinery, or another hand or two to help him. I used to try to help him but he always ran me off saying I couldn't do any man's work, just got in the way.

Ma and Pa were arguing when I got back to the house. I stood by the living room window and listened to them. I was scared by what Pa would do if he caught me but I just stooped down real low so they couldn't see me and listened some more. It was getting colder and I shifted now and then to keep warm. Pa was telling Ma how I was going to grow up with an education and make something of myself. Ma kept trying to say something but Pa just kept on: "I've always been tied down by things I don't know. We don't have much and now Bobby's growing up the same way. Well, as long as I'm alive and able to move, I'm going to try to give him a better life than I've had. I know I won't be around to see the results but I'm going to get him off to a good start."

Pa was getting upset again. He was tired from putting things together for the trip and Ma finally just turned around and walked toward the door. Pa stopped her and started talking real coddly-like: "Honey," he called her this time, "I just

Pa made his money planting potatoes and corn — all by hand and selling it to the people in town.

want something better for Bobby, for you, and all of us." Ma acted like she understood what he was talking about.

She went on to the door and I was afraid she was going to find me. She called my name. I waited a little and let her call it a few more times before I answered. I came around the corner of the house and handed her the empty hogwash container. She told me to wash up and get to bed. It was a little early but I didn't feel like disagreeing with her.

I tried to sleep but images of Grandpa and the house, the fields, and Grandma floated around in my brain like balloons, so light and bouncing and bumping into each other. A cutting wind could be heard, racing around the house, and huge black clouds slid across the sky, covering the light of the full moon. I remembered that I hadn't said good-night to Grandpa. It was still early and maybe he was awake. I tiptoed to his and Grandma's room. Grandma was asleep. Grandpa was lying there, wide awake, just looking into the darkness. He heard me and called my name lowly. I whispered, "I just wanted to say good-night." I hugged him then and started to cry. I don't know why but I didn't want to leave him there. All alone with no one to talk to. I could hear Grandma moan now and then in her sleep and turn over in her bed. Grandpa told me I had better leave and not wake her up.

I went back to bed and thought of Grandpa and his secret. Maybe it was something he was going to come up with that would keep us from leaving. Maybe he was going to show Pa something and make him change his mind. I felt better knowing he was going to do something; that he had a secret was enough for me. I knew Grandpa wouldn't lie to me, not something as serious as this. I thought about what Monday morning would be like. It would be early and Pa

18   would have everything ready to go. Ma and Grandma would be saying good-by and all of a sudden Grandpa would show his secret. Everyone would look at it, like it was some kind of a rare and precious jewel, and they'd start laughing and hugging and kissing each other because we didn't have to leave and Grandpa would be trying to tell us he had this secret all along but was just waiting to show it to us at the right time.

Rolling on the ground, shouting with happiness, and so proud of Grandpa, I wouldn't be able to keep all this inside of me. I would run across the fields shouting with all my might, "We don't have to go! We can stay with Grandpa and Grandma. We're still one family. We can stay!" I would run back the other way, past the house and down by the creek. I would run into the water, splash it all over me and feel so happy and glad that Grandpa hadn't lied to me.

I awoke the next morning late. The room was dark and the wind sounded like it was going to tear the house down. I sat on the bed and one big word popped into my mind: Sunday. I couldn't believe it. Still in my night clothes, I burst into the kitchen—and there Ma and Grandpa were getting ready for breakfast. Ma told me to wash and get ready to eat and then her next words almost knocked me over: "Get ready to leave too. A bad storm's moving in and we're leaving a day early. Pa's gone into town to tell those other people to come on out. Your Grandma's terribly sick so I don't want you making any unnecessary noise. Do you hear me?" I managed to utter "Yes." I sat down at the breakfast table but couldn't eat. I just stared at Grandpa, pleading and begging silently, with my eyes, for him to do something, anything. Tears were streaming down my face but no one even acted like I was alive, like I was even sitting there.

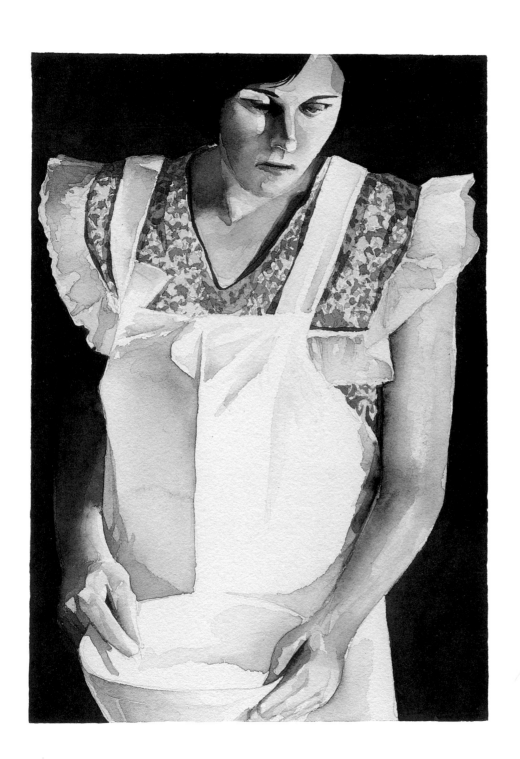

Ma and Grandpa were getting ready for breakfast. Ma told me to wash and get ready to eat.

I got up and told them I wasn't hungry. Ma started yelling at me and Grandpa told her to leave me alone. I went to my room and started packing my things in an old cardboard box I always found other uses for than to pack things in. Sleet could now be heard on the window and it seemed a little colder. I was again pleading inside to Grandpa to show his secret so we wouldn't have to leave but I wasn't in a daydream anymore. This was real and I began to think he didn't have a secret at all. I had to try real hard not to think this.

I heard Pa come in. Cussing and raising his voice, he asked if we all were ready. Ma came into my room just as I was stuffing the last of my socks into the bulging box. She looked at me and then I noticed what she was looking at. I wasn't dressed. She turned and said to Pa: "Go ahead and get the other boxes into the car. I'll help Bobby get dressed." While she was pulling on my arms and twisting my legs and feet this way and that, I was looking out the window—big fluffy flakes of snow were falling against it.

I could hear Pa come back in. He said something to Grandpa about a doctor coming for Grandma and how the new people were also on their way. I was thinking about missing church with Grandpa, not being able to visit my favorite spot by the creek, and Grandma being sick. And us just up and leaving like this. I stared at Grandpa. He stooped down and he kissed me. Pa picked up the big box of my clothes and Ma and Grandpa were saying good-by. We all went into the living room and Grandpa leaned over again and hugged me. I didn't hug him back—I couldn't. And then he told me something: "Remember our secret," and I saw a twinkle in his eyes and a tear start to slide down his cheek. "Good-by, Bobby," I heard him say as I ran out the open door into the cold and snowy front yard. Ma had the back car door open and I jumped in amid the boxes and buried my face against the backseat and cried.

Ma got in and I heard the car start. As we went down the lane, I pressed my tear-stained face against the back window and wiped away the steam. One picture sticks in my mind: Grandpa standing in the yard waving. The snow was almost hiding the trees and woods. The house was barely visible—a thin stream of smoke trailing a few feet into the snowy sky. Then there were the cows and I knew I was leaving all that I had ever seen from the house and was starting on a long trip. But this time, not to town; a trip further than that, a trip further than I'd ever taken before.

I stayed glued to the window until all I could see was blurred snow and trees passing steadily as we went down the road. There's a fork in the road where one road takes you into town, the one on the left. We took the one to the right. Pa put the heater on and Ma shifted in the front seat to get more comfortable and see where Pa was driving. I was getting hungry now but I didn't dare say anything because I knew Ma would just yell at how I didn't eat my breakfast.

With all the new places I was seeing, I felt like I was asleep and in a dream. The windows kept getting steamed up and Pa finally got fed up with me going from door to door, stumbling and shoving the boxes around, trying to see something. There was nothing but snow, trees, mountains, and an emptiness inside me that I couldn't even begin to explain.

I slept a little but Ma woke me up to give me a couple pieces of fried chicken and a glass of ice-cold milk. It was still daylight. We were at some gas station and restaurant. Snow was still falling but the mountains were gone. I turned around

The snow was almost hiding the trees and woods. The house was barely visible — a thin stream of smoke trailing a few feet into the snowy sky.

in the backseat and looked for them. I couldn't see anything much, just snow and a little piece of the highway. A man was putting gas into the car and I guessed Pa was inside the station. Ma was telling me to eat the chicken before it got cold and as hungry as I was, it didn't take much coaxing for that.

I noticed a big clock in the restaurant window: three-thirty. Ma saw me looking at it and told me that Pa said we should be there in another hour, if we didn't get lost or anything. The snow was getting deep on the grass but the road was clear. Ma said we were on a main highway but she didn't know how the roads would be by the time we got to where we were going. She was saying how early this snow was and we were lucky to get out as soon as we did. I was busy eating until I suddenly thought of something and I said it out loud: "Do you think the doctor will be able to get in to see Grandma?" I noticed Ma suddenly become aware of what I had said. She said she was sure the new people would make it there all right and they could do just as much as anyone else could to get the doctor.

Pa opened the door and asked me if I had to use the bathroom. He showed me a door on the side of the building and told me to come straight back to the car and not to linger. He looked at the sky and just shook his head. When I got back to the car, they were ready to go. The snow was so clean-looking and the air was so fresh and cold. I wanted to play some but that was out of the question. Pa had a little cake waiting for me after I again settled in my nest between the boxes. I watched the town go by and saw a few people I'd never seen before. The same dull countryside came again though and I fell asleep a second time.

Ma was shaking me just as we were pulling into the lane

of one of the most beautiful homes I had ever seen. The snow had stopped but boy was it ever deep. Pa tried to go on up the lane but the car just took one big leap and the motor quit running. Ma was asking Pa if he was sure this was the right house and Pa told her he was sure.

A man came out on the porch and stared at us. Two little boys followed him and then yet another kid came out, a girl, and they stared at us. Pa walked up the lane a little ways until he could hear what the man was saying. Pa nodded his head a couple of times and turned and started walking back to the car. The snow came up to his knees and Ma and I were going to have to walk through it. Pa took two big boxes and Ma took one. They didn't give me any, probably because I couldn't carry it anyway.

We went inside the big house and a woman came out of the kitchen. Pa shook hands with the owner and then with the woman. Ma then did the same. We kids just stood there looking at each other. I stood close to Pa because there were three of them to just me and they looked mean. The man told Pa that the second floor was ours. It had a kitchen, two bedrooms, a living room, and a bathroom. Pa told us to go up and get settled and he and the other man went into a big room to talk.

The boys watched Ma and me go up the steps. I had to carry one of the boxes Pa had carried in; I left the other behind, I'd just have to come back and get it. When I came back, the two boys were there but the girl had gone some-where. I asked them if they went to school. "Sure. Just started," one of them replied. "Have to walk about a half mile," the other one said. They looked almost like twins. "Both of you in the same grade?" I asked. "Yeah, first grade.

We kids just stood there looking at each other. I stood close to Pa because there were three of them to just me and they looked mean.

Our sister doesn't start until next year," the other boy told me.

Ma was yelling for the last box, so I had to go. They watched me climb the stairs again. Ma told me the man's name was Mr. Spade Henderson and Pa would be working for him. She had already found some food and was preparing supper. I was thinking out loud: "Today's Sunday. The mail goes tomorrow. I'm going to write a letter to Grandpa!" I was hurrying to my bedroom when I passed this beautiful desk with all kinds of ink and pens and stuff on it. There also was a light on it, for writing at night, I guessed. My eye caught something. It was a dull shade of yellow paper with funny curls around the edges. It felt slippery and smooth. I wondered what it would be like to write on it. Maybe Grandpa hadn't seen any of it before either.

I stole a piece of it and hurried on to my room, dug down in the box for a pencil and started my letter: "Dear Grandpa. We made it all right. This is a big house with two layers. We have the top layer. They have three kids, two boys and a girl. Pa got stuck in the snow down at the foot of the lane." I was writing too big and then I noticed that there wasn't much room left to finish. The little curls took up a lot of room. I used the remaining space for these words: "Write soon. I miss you. I wish you were here." I just signed it "Bobby."

Now I needed an envelope. I returned to the table and found one but there was writing at the top left-hand corner of it. Ma came in and caught me. I told her I had written to Grandpa and needed an envelope. She looked at the envelope and said it would be all right. It was Mr. Henderson's own address at the top corner. "Be sure and tell your Grandpa this is where to write and tell him Pa and I said hello."

I went back to my room and looked at the envelope and then the letter. I didn't think there was enough room to put everything she had said on it. Then something simple hit me. I turned the page over and there was one whole new side. I immediately set to writing on this side: "P. S.," I began, "Ma and Pa said hello to you. Write to the address in the corner. That is the man who owns the place. Maybe you can come visit us sometime." I was writing big again and the space was gone. I turned the letter over and reread the first page. At the bottom I added the word "over." I sealed it up and just sat there for a minute looking at our new address. Ma came in again and told me to address the envelope. She had found a stamp and would mail it tomorrow. I had to ask Ma where to write and she told me to write Grandpa's name and put R. F. D. and she would finish it.

It was starting to get dark outside and I looked out the window, longing once again to see the mountains. Snow drifted down the hills and played circles around the fence posts. I could still see Pa's car down at the end of the lane. There they were, the mountains—far away, so dark and clear. The wind whipped around the corner of the house and I wondered if Grandpa and Grandma were warm. I wondered how the man was treating them and if the doctor ever got there to see Grandma. I wondered what they were doing now, how deep the snow was there and if the new man was too lazy to shovel the snow from the lane so they could go to town, or go to church, or even to go get the mail.

Ma called me for supper. Pa was back and telling what a good deal he was getting. He said Mr. Henderson owned from three hundred fifty to four hundred acres of land here and Pa would be in charge and would draw four hundred

P.S. Ma AND
HELLO.
TO THE Add
CORNER
THE MAN
THE PLACE

COME
Someti

I turned the page over and there was one whole new side. I immediately set to writing on this side: "P.S.," I began, "Ma and Pa said hello to you. Write to the address in the corner. That is the man who owns the place. Maybe you can come visit us sometime."

dollars a month if he kept the land production up to its full   33
output. He was hugging Ma and they were laughing and
carrying on and then he pulled out the biggest roll of money
I'd ever seen. "He gave me my first month's pay in advance!"
shouted Pa and he hugged Ma again. I just stood there. I
couldn't believe this was happening to us. Pa, a nice job, Ma,
happy again, and me, going to school. I jumped up and down
myself and started hugging Ma too. Just the three of us.

We finished supper and sat around the living room.
There was this great-big radio and Pa turned it on and found
some music. He and Ma sat together holding hands. I always
felt so good when I saw Ma and Pa like that. He was telling
her the school was a half mile down the road and I'd walk
with the other boys tomorrow, snow or no snow. He was
saying he would send some money to Grandpa and Grandma
and maybe we could visit them soon—maybe spring. I
almost floated on the air when I heard this, actually going
back someday, maybe soon, to the old homeplace, to see
Grandpa and Grandma.

A week passed, two weeks, and I came running into the
house every evening after school looking for a letter from
Grandpa. And then it came. It was addressed to me—Master
Bobby was printed in Grandpa's own writing. Underneath
was Care of Mr. Spade·Henderson, R.F.D. 2, and then the city,
which I hadn't learned to pronounce yet, and Virginia.
"Grandpa's done it!" I shouted as I bounded up the stairs to
my room. All the two weeks of going to school, studying
hard, going to church and sometimes helping Pa on Satur-
days had been worth it—Grandpa had written!

I studied the handwriting on the envelope a minute
before I ripped it open. I used to always like to delay things

like that, to make them last a little longer than they usually would. The letter began, "Dear Bobby. I am so glad and happy for you. The paper you used is beautiful. The people there must really be rich and nice. I'm so afraid you're going to forget me. Grandma's gone, she died a day after you all left. Wouldn't eat or do nothing. I didn't know what to do. Doctor said she just didn't want to live any more."

I couldn't believe my eyes. It was like I was reading someone else's letter. It wasn't meant for me. Grandma couldn't die and leave Grandpa. They were made for each other. When two people are made like that, one of them just doesn't up and leave the other. I thought of Ma and Pa then.

"Now I don't know what to do," he wrote on. "The people here are like strangers. The doctor had her buried and now I'm all alone. Sometimes I wish I could have gone with her." It wasn't even signed. He had kept his promise though. I thought of how hard it must have been for him to write that letter, the courage it must have took and how it must have tore at his insides telling me all that.

Years went by and I moved up to high school. Mr. Henderson sold Pa a plot of land and we built a home of our own on it. Pa said I would be getting married soon and we would be needing more room and a place of our own. I had forgotten about Grandpa until one day a letter came from a Mr. Joseph Ridley. He explained that the old man who lived with him had just died and among his things a letter was found with my name and Mr. Spade Henderson's address on it. He explained that he was a hired hand that had moved there eight years before and had sort of looked out for the old man. "I am sending his only possession in a box which I will mail to you tomorrow because I have to go into town to weigh it for

He had kept my picture somewhere else. I wondered what he had done with it, where it could be.

postage." That was all he had written. Grandpa was gone. He couldn't possibly have been talking about someone else. I thought about his secret—what he had taught me and what he had said: "Love your father and mother," he told me so many times. "Go to church every Sunday with them and take them with you when you're old enough." His words now echoed ever so clear. I had done that. It was all a part of Grandpa's "secret," how to live, let live and enjoy life; it was about being loved and loving one another.

The package arrived the next day. I opened it very carefully because it seemed to be something fragile and very delicate. There it was—the big picture frame that had set for the many years on the bureau top in Grandpa's room. I examined the pictures, one by one. Grandma first, Grandpa second, then Pa and, lastly, Ma. He had kept my picture somewhere else. I wondered what he had done with it, where it could be. I looked at the pictures again, this time together, as a whole family.

Ma and Pa turned and walked away, leaving me holding the picture frame reverently in my hand. I started crying and these words came to me then: "This is my heritage, my past, and part of my whole life. Grandpa kept it on his bureau all these years. How it must have tormented him when he found himself looking at them when he felt lonely and empty inside." But then maybe he wasn't tormented at all; I think Grandpa had a range of knowledge and power far beyond my small world and what I was capable of seeing.

We never got around to going back there when Grandpa was alive, though Pa was always talking about it, and now there was nothing to go back for, just memories; but maybe, someday before I die, I'm going back to live there again.

Born to a seventeen-year-old mother, Truman Capote spent the first seven years of his life with aunts and cousins, including Marie Rudisill, his mother's younger sister. Bud, an elderly cousin, is the model for Grandpa in this story, as his sister Sook was for the elderly Cousin in A Christmas Memory.

On a visit to Mrs. Rudisill in 1946, Capote, then twenty-two and at work on Other Voices, Other Rooms, *wrote* I Remember Grandpa *as a gift for his aunt because cousin Bud was a favorite of hers. When she asked what she was to do with the story, the young author said, "Anything in this world you want to do with it — do. Why, someday I might even be famous."*

And so he was. After Capote's death in 1984, Mrs. Rudisill found the long-forgotten manuscript among her papers. She felt that it should be published because, "The early writings of anybody are the purest." For her, I Remember Grandpa *captures both the young Capote's love for the cousin who urged the child to think of him as a grandfather and the young man's eventual disappointment in family life and its promised joys.*

For Marie Rudisill, this is a sweet, touching story that reveals with clarity and simplicity the roots of Truman Capote's life, a gift she felt she must share.